Very Tricky, Alfie Atkins

Written and illustrated by Gunilla Bergström

Translated by
Elisabeth Kallick Dyssegaard

R&S
BOOKS

Stockholm New York London Adelaide Toronto

Here is Alfie Atkins, five years old.
There are two things he likes
most of all. The best is when
the grownups play with him.
But Daddy doesn't always want
to play. The next best thing is the
coat closet, because that's where
Daddy keeps his toolbox. But Alfie
never gets to borrow it.
"No, no, you could hurt yourself
with the saw," says Daddy. "Play
with Sissel instead."
Sissel is Alfie's cat.

But some days Daddy wants to relax and be left in peace. He might want to read the paper or watch TV and not be with Alfie at all. That's when Alfie might possibly be able to borrow the toolbox! When daddies want to be left in peace, they don't pay too much attention to what you do. That's what it is like today.

Daddy is reading the newspaper.

"Can I borrow the toolbox?" asks Alfie.

"Mmm," says Daddy. "But be careful with the saw."

Alfie gets the toolbox. He gets some wood, too. It's heavy. Now he is carrying nails and tacks and the wrench and the hammer and the screwdriver and the ruler and the saw. Daddy is reading.

"You may not use the saw," he says from behind the paper.

Alfie doesn't touch the saw.

He begins with the hammer
and some nails.
Bam, bam, bam.
Daddy reads.
"You're not touching the
saw, are you?" he asks from
behind the newspaper. But
Alfie just has the hammer!
He's not touching the saw.

He can see that he doesn't have enough wood.
"Can I take the broken stool,
Daddy?" asks Alfie.
"Mmm," says Daddy from
behind the newspaper. "But
don't touch the saw!"
Alfie gets the stool.
He doesn't touch the saw.

Now he has to measure as well.
"Can I use the yardstick, Daddy?"
he asks.
Daddy reads and reads.
"Mmm," he answers after a long time.
"But watch out for the saw," he adds.
Alfie takes the yardstick and measures.
He doesn't take the saw.

Now Alfie misses,
and the hammer comes
down on his thumb
and it hurts a lot.
But he doesn't say
anything.

Now Alfie misses, and the nail becomes
crooked and has to be pulled out.
"I need to use the pliers, Daddy!" he says.
Daddy just keeps reading.
"Can I borrow the pliers, Daddy?"
asks Alfie again.
"Mmm," says Daddy finally.
"As long as you don't touch
the saw . . ."
Alfie takes the pliers and
pulls out the nail.
But he doesn't touch the saw.

Then Alfie works for a long time
without saying a thing.
Only the hammer can be heard.
Bam, bam, bam.
What an odd thing he is building.
Will it be a fence? Or a fort?
Now it's finished.
"Daddy, look what I've built!" yells Alfie.
Daddy reads and reads.
"Oh, how nice," he finally says—but doesn't
even look in Alfie's direction.
"You're not touching the saw, are you?" he just asks.
Alfie is not.
Because he *can't.*
He can't reach that far now.

Look! It's turned into a helicopter.
Alfie is pretending to fly across the jungle.
It's the middle of the night. The moon is shining.
He sees strange forests and animals—elephants
and tigers and palm trees. And Sissel has turned
into a lion!
That's when Daddy rustles the paper and says,
"You aren't touching the saw, are you?"
But that's exactly what Alfie is planning to do because . . .

. . . Alfie lands in the jungle
by the lion, and—oh no!
The big, dangerous lion is coming closer!
"Help!" yells Alfie. "I'm stuck
and the lion is going to get me.
I NEED THE SAW!"
"Not the saw," says Daddy
from behind the newspaper.
But Alfie
keeps
yelling.
"Help!
Help!"

And now Daddy looks up from the newspaper.
"Alfie! Alfie, what have you *done*?"
"Built a helicopter and landed it
in the jungle," says Alfie.
"But you're stuck!
How are you going to get out?"
yells Daddy worriedly.
Alfie looks sneaky. He says,
"If I can have the saw,
then I can saw my way out."
"No," says Daddy. "The saw
is dangerous."
But Alfie insists that the lion
is also dangerous, so he has
to get out of his helicopter.
Daddy looks at the helicopter
and thinks it looks nice and says,
"Can I come along? Then we
can escape from the lion together."

And that's exactly what Alfie wants most of all!
Daddy climbs up. Alfie steers.
Finally Daddy is playing.
They fly far away and high up and see lots
of things—boats and cars and airplanes and clouds.
They fly for a long, long time. Until . . .

23

. . . the evening news begins.
Then Daddy has to get off.
They land at home in the living room.
Daddy climbs out and says,
"Wait a moment, Alfie. I'll help you get out. I just
need to fetch the saw."
But now it's Alfie who yells, "No, no! Not the saw.
You can hurt yourself. And I can . . .

". . . I *can* get out! I was just pretending
that I was stuck."
Yes, look—Alfie climbs out!
He is happy. Because Daddy played with him.
And because he got to borrow the toolbox.
Daddy just laughs. "Ha, ha, ha!
Very tricky, Alfie Atkins!"

26

Rabén & Sjögren Bokförlag, Stockholm
www.raben.se

Alfie's home page:
www.alfons.se

Translation copyright © 2005 by Rabén & Sjögren Bokförlag
All rights reserved
Originally published in Sweden by Rabén & Sjögren under the title *Aja baja Alfons Åberg*
Copyright © 1972 by Gunilla Bergström
Library of Congress Control Number: 2003098280
Printed in Denmark
First American edition, 2005
ISBN 91-29-66152-8